THE MUSIC IN ME

Sophy Henn

SIMON & SCHUSTER

London New York Sydney Toronto New Delhi

D1420073

I've got rhythm in my **fingers** . . .

. . . I've got rhythm in my **toes**.

And there's a beat inside my belly that

just **grows**

and **grows**

and grows!

I'm chock-a-block with music,
and guess what?

You are, too!

All kinds of different rhythms
go to make up me and you.

Your music's always playing.
And it's very often changing.
It can make you feel all
kinds of wrong and right.

You see, some days . . .

. . . I get a beat, I get a rhythm,
that's so happy I could **burst**.

I smile and hop and skip and jump
and greet the day headfirst.

It's like everything
is sunshine –
you can't help but
have a fun time

and **WOWSERS,**

there is nothing wrong with that.

THEN . . .

. . . on other days . . .

. . . the rhythm . . .

slows . . .

. . . down.

Everything feels heavy
and the beat's just crawling, creeping.

My legs are made of stone and
I'm sure I should be sleeping.

But my eyes are wide,
    wide open.
        And I feel a little frozen
    and, HEAVENS,
        will this day just NEVER END?

    BUT . . .

            . . . maybe . . .

. . . next I'll hear a marching
beat, and march is what I must.

So I stomp along with purpose,
I am brave
and true
and just.

And even if it looks to me
that everybody else I see
is marching straight
the other way . . .

ON
I
MARCH.

Until I can't
march any
more . . .

And my music might get swoony
and all dreamy and I fly.

I'm soaring and I'm looping,

gliding right across the sky.

I'm made of stardust and I shine,
it's like the universe is mine
and absolutely everything's alright.

But then . . .

. . . some days,

it's not . . .

And my rhythm goes all jumpy,
and I think too many thoughts.

I'm everything and nothing,
all at once and out of sorts.

I don't know what I feel like,
and I just can't put a foot right.

The beat is **zigzag-zigging**
all around.

And then . . .

. . . perhaps . . .

. . . it all
GETS LOUD.

My music is a **GIANT NOISE**,
a wall of angry sound.
Fighting other rhythms in a
noisy battleground.

And I feel like I'm ginormous,
and my mighty roar's humongous.

Big and loud I stand apart . . .

I feel alone.

So . . .

. . . I'll seek out others' lovely songs
and sing in harmony.
Or sometimes others might just want
to sing along with me.

Whatever way it comes about,
it's MAGIC when it all works out.

It feels so rainbow good

and I am pink!

But . . .

. . . sometimes I lose MY rhythm,
or sing someone else's song,
I know it's not my music
and it feels not right but wrong.

And then I start to worry,
even though it will not help me.

If I **stop** and listen
it will come along.

So I **stop** . . .

and **listen**. Shhhhhh . . .

. . . THERE IT IS!

And I'm so happy that I've found it,
even if it's **fast** or **slow**.
Because it's mine, it's just for me,
and it's the bestest song I know.

I will march to my own drum beat.
It's a beat that I just can't cheat
'cause the person I'd be cheating would be **me**.

See?

And now . . .

. . . my beat is on the up and up,
my smile is just the **MOST.**

I'm the leader of a BIG parade,
first past the winning post.

It's almost like my shoes have wings.
I've all the joy that playtime brings,

and GEE it's super great to just be **me**!

So . . .

. . . I might not hit the notes quite right,
sometimes I'll lose the beat.
But I'll listen to my rhythm
as my rhythm's super sweet.

And if I stay true to my song,
then I really can't go far wrong.

It's **MY** music

and my music
makes me, **ME**.

for
peteselby
who quite
likes music.

xxx

SIMON & SCHUSTER

First published in Great Britain in 2022 by Simon & Schuster UK Ltd
1st Floor, 222 Gray's Inn Road, London WC1X 8HB

A CIP catalogue record for this book is available from
the British Library upon request

ISBN: 978-1-4711-9426-9 (HB)
ISBN: 978-1-4711--9425-2 (PB)
ISBN: 978-1-4711-9427-6 (eBook)
ISBN: 978-1-3985-1441-6 (eAudio)

Printed in China
1 3 5 7 9 10 8 6 4 2